Karen's Little Sister

Also in the Babysitters Little Sister series:

Look out for:

Karen's Little Sister

Ann M. Martin

Illustrations by Susan Tang

Hippo Books
Scholastic Children's Books
London

Scholastic Children's Books,
Scholastic Publications Ltd,
7-9 Pratt Street, London NW1 0AE, UK

Scholastic Inc.,
730 Broadway, New York, NY 10003, USA

Scholastic Canada Ltd,
123 Newkirk Road, Richmond Hill,
Ontario, Canada L4C 3G5

Ashton Scholastic Pty Ltd,
P O Box 579, Gosford, New South Wales,
Australia

Ashton Scholastic Ltd,
Private Bag 1, Penrose, Auckland,
New Zealand

First published in the USA by Scholastic Inc., 1989
First published in the UK by Scholastic Publications Ltd, 1992

Copyright © Ann M. Martin, 1989

ISBN 0 590 55034 9

Typeset by A.J. Latham Ltd, Dunstable, Beds
Printed by Cox & Wyman Ltd, Reading, Berks

BABYSITTERS LITTLE SISTER is a trademark of Scholastic Inc.

10 9 8 7 6 5 4 3

This book is for
Ann and David,
Laura and Johnny,
Shortie the dachshund,
and, of course,
Blaze Midnight the rat.

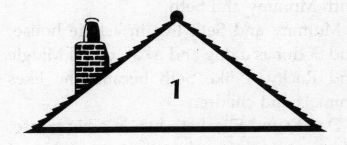

Rocky and Midgie

Hello. Here I am again. It's me, Karen Brewer. I'm six (*nearly* seven) years old. I have freckles, wear glasses and I have a little brother who is four. Once I broke my wrist and I had to have a plastercast on my arm.

Do you want to know the most interesting thing of all about me? I have *two* families. That's because a long time ago, my mummy and daddy got divorced and then they both got married again. Mummy married Seth, who is my stepfather and Daddy married Elizabeth, who is my stepmother. Most of the time, my brother Andrew and I live with Mummy and Seth.

Mummy and Seth live in a little house, and Seth has a dog and a cat, called Midgie and Rocky. I like Seth because he likes animals and children.

Daddy and Elizabeth live in a big house. That is a good thing because an awful lot of other people live there with them. To begin with, Elizabeth has four children. They are Sam and Charlie, who go to high school, and Kristy, who is thirteen. She is one of my favourite people in the world. The last one is David Michael. He is seven. He can be a pain in the neck. Sam, Charlie, and David Michael are my stepbrothers and Kristy is my stepsister. Another person at the big house is Nannie. Nannie is Elizabeth's mother, so she is sort of my grandmother.

Then there is Emily Michelle. Daddy and Elizabeth adopted her. She came from a faraway country called Vietnam. Emily is two and she is my adopted sister. Most of the time, I think of her as my little sister.

I call Andrew Andrew Two-Two and I call myself Karen Two-Two. I got the names from the title of a book my teacher once read to us. It was called *Jacob Two-Two Meets the Hooded Fang*.

Andrew and I are two-twos because we have two of almost everything. We have two families and two houses. (Andrew and I live at the big house every other weekend.) I have two stuffed cats, one at each house and I have two bikes, one at each house. Andrew and I have clothes and toys at each house. We also have two dogs and two cats — Rocky and Midgie are at the little house, and at the big house are Shannon the puppy and Boo-Boo, Daddy's fat old cat.

Do you know what I wish, though? I wish I had a pet of my own. Rocky and Midgie and Shannon and Boo-Boo really belong to other people. Rocky and Midgie are Seth's, Shannon is David Michael's, and Boo-Boo is Daddy's. Sometimes I pretend they are mine, though.

One night, Rocky and Midgie were in my room at the little house. We were playing a game so I had closed the door to keep them in.

I was the mother and Rocky and Midgie were my children.

"Come here, Rocky," I said. "It's time for you to get dressed."

I pulled Rocky into my lap. I tied a doll's bonnet on his head, which wasn't easy. "Mrow!" said Rocky.

"Hold still," I told him. "I have to put your — Midgie, get back in bed!" Midgie was supposed to be napping in my doll's bed.

He jumped out.

Rocky pawed at his bonnet until it came off. Then they both ran to the door.

"Oh, *drat!*" I cried.

"Karen, what's going on in there?" called Mummy.

"Nothing," I answered.

I opened my door. Rocky and Midgie flew into the hall and darted down the stairs.

"I wish," I said out loud, "that I had a pet of my *own.*"

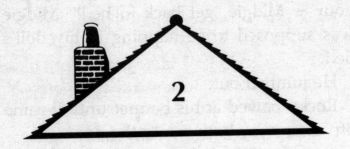

Emily Michelle

"Karen! Andrew! Are you ready to go to Daddy's?" asked Mummy.

It was a special Friday evening. It was a going-to-Daddy's Friday.

Andrew and I ran to Mummy in the kitchen. Our bags were already packed. One nice thing about being a two-two is that you hardly have to remember to take anything with you when you go from one house to the other. You only need a few things that fit into a bag.

"We're ready!" I said.

Mummy had put her coat on. Her car keys were in one hand and her handbag was in the other.

Mummy and I look alike as we both have blonde hair and freckles and wear glasses. Andrew only looks a little like us; he has blonde hair, too, but not as many freckles, and no glasses.

"Let's go!" said Andrew.

Mummy drove us to the big house. "Goodbye!" she called as Daddy let us in the front door. "Have fun! See you on Sunday! I love you!"

"Love you, too!" said Andrew and I.

And suddenly we were in the big house. We were surrounded by people and noise and excitement.

"Hi, Professor," David Michael said to me.

That's what he started calling me when I got glasses. It's not an unkind nickname; it's a nice one.

Daddy walked into the hall carrying Emily. Emily was whining and crying and

7

rubbing one of her ears. She does that a lot.

"What's wrong with Emily?" I asked.

"Yes. Why is she crying?" asked Andrew.

"We don't think she's feeling very well," Daddy answered. "We think she might have another earache."

Daddy leaned over and kissed Andrew and me. He couldn't hug us, though, because his arms were full of Emily. Daddy always used to hug us when we came for the weekend.

Emily didn't stop crying. She cried while the rest of us ate supper. Daddy and Elizabeth and Nannie had been invited to a dinner party, but now they couldn't decide whether to go. Daddy kept feeling Emily's forehead and saying, "I think she's got a temperature. Maybe we shouldn't leave."

Finally Elizabeth took Emily's temperature. It was normal.

Nobody paid a bit of attention to Andrew or me. I was furious. We don't see the big-house people very often. It wasn't fair that Emily got all the attention.

I looked at Andrew. He looked at me. We weren't happy. Andrew used to be the youngest at the big house and I used to be the youngest girl. Now Emily is the baby she's ruined everything.

Anyway, Daddy and Elizabeth and Nannie finally went to their dinner party, Charlie and Sam went to a basketball game at their school and Kristy was left babysitting.

Usually, I love it when Kristy babysits. She is a good sitter. She and her friends have even started a group called the Babysitters Club. But that night was no fun. Emily cried and cried so Kristy rocked her and read to her and spent an hour trying to get her to go to sleep.

She didn't even have time to read me a bedtime story.

I decided that I didn't like having a little sister.

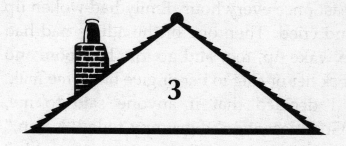

The Grumpy Morning

When I woke up the next morning, I was in a very bad mood. I felt grumpy all over.

"I hope Emily behaves herself today," I said crossly to Moosie. Moosie is my stuffed cat. I always sleep with him and with Tickly, which is half of my special blue blanket. (The other half is at Mummy's). "If Emily doesn't behave herself, maybe I will just go back to Mummy's. At Mummy's, I don't have a little sister."

I hadn't slept well the night before. Who

can sleep with so much noise? All night, at least once every hour, Emily had woken up and cried. Then one of the adults had had to wake up, too, and go into her room and rock her or sing to her or give her some milk.

I decided that if anyone said to me, "Goodness, you're grumpy today, Karen," I would answer, "That's because I couldn't sleep last night, thanks to Emily. She made too much noise."

I rolled out of bed and got dressed. Sometimes I like to wear skirts, even on Saturdays. So I put on a blue skirt and a pink-and-white striped top. Then I pulled on pink socks and my white trainers.

I brushed my hair, made my bed and put Moosie and Tickly on top of my bed.

I thought about Goosie (my other stuffed cat) and the other half of Tickly over at Mummy's house. Maybe I would be sleeping with *them* that night.

Finally I went downstairs. In the kitchen I found Daddy, Elizabeth, Nannie, Kristy, and Emily. All the boys were still asleep.

12

Emily was in her high chair and she was crying as usual.

Nannie put her hand on Emily's forehead and said, "Now I think she does have a temperature."

Elizabeth said, "I think she should definitely go to the doctor. Her ear is still bothering her. I'm sure she has another ear infection."

Daddy said, "I'll call the doctor right now."

No one noticed me, so finally I said in a very loud voice, "GOOD MORNING!"

Emily cried harder.

Daddy said, "Karen, keep your voice down, please. Emily isn't feeling well."

I sat down at the table in a huff.

I crossed my arms and stared at Emily Michelle. Be quiet, be quiet, be quiet, I thought. But Emily wouldn't stop crying.

"Poor baby," said Elizabeth. She lifted Emily out of her high chair and gave her a hug.

Daddy called the doctor. "Okay," he said when he had hung up the phone. "Doctor Dellenkamp can see Emily at eleven."

"That's great," replied Elizabeth. "I'll take her."

"And I'll go with you," said Kristy.

Oh no! I wanted to play with Kristy that morning.

Elizabeth put Emily back in her high chair and gave her a bowl of cereal.

14

"May I have some cereal too, please?" I asked.

"Oh, Karen, I'm sorry," said Elizabeth. "I didn't know you wanted any. I've finished the packet."

Drat! I stuck my tongue out at Emily.

Just then, Emily knocked over her bowl of cereal. The milk splashed on my blouse.

"Emily!" I cried. "Bad girl!"

Emily burst into tears.

Daddy scolded me.

I couldn't wait for Emily to leave for her doctor's visit.

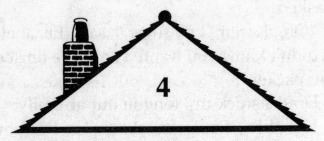

Shannon, Boo-Boo,
and Pat the Cat

Emily was ruining the weekend.

It wasn't fair. When the clock said twenty to eleven, I breathed a huge sigh of relief. That was because Elizabeth, Emily, and Kristy left the house then. They were on their way to Dr Dellenkamp's.

I didn't understand one thing, though. Why did Kristy have to go? She sees Emily every day because she lives with her. But she only sees me two weekends every month. What was so special about Emily and her ear? She was always getting earaches.

I waved sadly to Kristy as Elizabeth drove down the street.

Then I sat on our front steps. It was nice and peaceful without Emily and her squawking and crying, but I wanted to do something. I walked around to the back garden. I found David Michael, Andrew, Shannon, and Boo-Boo there.

Good! I thought. I can play with one of the pets.

Shannon was busy chasing sticks that the boys were throwing, so I would have to play with Boo-Boo. Boo-Boo was in Daddy's herb garden.

He was asleep.

"Boo-Boo," I whispered. "Boo-Boo. . . *Boo-Boo*. . . BOO-BOO!"

Boo-Boo stirred, but he didn't even open an eye.

I shook him gently. "Wake up! Wake up!"

"Grrr," growled Boo-Boo. That was cat talk for, "Go away and let me sleep." Emily had even kept Boo-Boo awake during the night.

I left Boo-Boo alone. Who wants to play with someone who doesn't want to play with you? Now I really, really, really wanted a pet of my own.

Then I had an idea. I ran inside and phoned Hannie Papadakis. Hannie is my big-house best friend because she lives over the road from us. (I have a little-house best friend, too. Her name is Nancy Dawes and she lives next door to Mummy. Hannie and Nancy and I are in the same class at school.)

"Hannie?" I said. "Do you want to come over?. . . You do? Oh, good. Can you bring Pat? I promise that Boo-Boo won't bother her." Pat is Hannie's kitten and I love her. She is a very good kitten, unlike other cats I can think of who won't wake up or won't wear dolls' bonnets.

So Hannie came over, carrying Pat in her arms.

We sat in my front garden.

"Hi, Pat," I said, "Hi, Pitty-Pat."

Pat purred and purred.

"What shall we play?" Hannie asked me.

I thought for a moment. "Let's play house. I'll be the mother, you be the father, and Pat will be our baby."

"Okay," said Hannie.

But Pat was frisking around the garden. She didn't look as if she was going to want to be our baby.

"Wait," I said. "I have a better idea. Look at those dandelions growing by the pavement. Let's make Pat some dandelion jewellery."

So we did. We made her four little bracelets and a necklace.

Just as we were finishing the necklace, Elizabeth's car pulled into the drive.

"There are Kristy and Emily and Elizabeth!" I cried, jumping up. "I have to go and find out what the doctor said about Emily's ear."

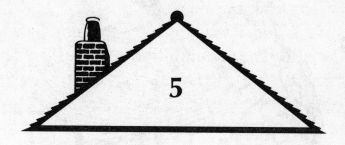

Emily's Ears

When I asked Elizabeth about Emily's ear, she just said, "At lunchtime I'll tell everybody what the doctor said."

It was almost lunchtime anyway, so Hannie took Pat home. Pat looked lovely in her dandelion jewellery.

My brothers and Kristy and I helped make lunch. We took everything out of the refrigerator, put it on the worktop, and made our own lunches. When we sat down to eat, the whole family was at the long kitchen table. Daddy sat at one end and

Elizabeth sat at the other. Kristy, Andrew, Nannie, and I were squeezed onto one side, and Sam, Charlie, and David Michael sat opposite us. Emily was in her high chair, next to Elizabeth.

"Well," said Elizabeth, "I have an announcement to make."

Everybody stopped eating and looked at her.

"Is the announcement about Emily?" I asked.

22

"Yes," replied Elizabeth. "The doctor said she does have another ear infection. Then she said that Emily has had too many ear infections. She wants to put some special tubes in her ears."

"Tubes in her ears!" exclaimed David Michael.

"Yes. They'll help drain fluid when she gets a cold, so that it won't infect her ears. When she's a little older, the tubes will be taken out."

"Yuck!" I said.

"How do they put the tubes in her ears?" asked Andrew.

"Emily will have to go into hospital," Elizabeth replied. "Just for a night. She'll have an operation in the morning and the surgeon will put the tubes in. It's actually pretty simple. Emily can come home later that day. Doctor Dellenkamp wants to do this in two weeks' time, when Emily's earache has cleared up."

Oh, that's great, I thought. That's just great. Guess when two weeks' time would be? It would be Andrew's and my next visit to the big house. Everyone would be fussing over Emily then. Some of the adults would probably want to stay at the hospital with her. Maybe *all* of the adults would want to stay at the hospital. Maybe even *Kristy* would want to.

What a fun weekend that would be.

I put my fork down. I was very cross. Why did Emily get all the attention? She was even going to stay in hospital. I didn't have to stay in hospital when I broke my wrist. I just went to casualty for a while.

I was very very upset.

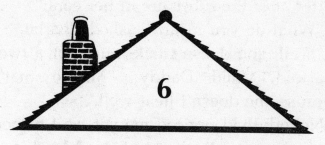

6

"Hey, Everybody! Look at Me!"

There was only one good thing about the rest of the weekend. That was that Emily stopped crying and rubbing her ear. Dr Dellenkamp had given her some medicine and she started to feel better straight away.

But nobody could stop talking about Emily.

On Saturday afternoon, I walked into the study. Daddy and Charlie and Emily were there. There was a baseball game on TV, but Daddy and Charlie weren't watching it. Daddy was holding Emily in his lap and saying, "Maybe Emily's speech will get better after the tubes are in her ears."

"What do you mean?" asked Charlie.

"Well, she doesn't talk much for a two-year-old," said Daddy. "Maybe that's because she doesn't hear well."

Nobody had noticed me yet, so I turned a somersault into the study and landed at Daddy's feet.

"Look at me!" I cried.

Daddy said, "Very nice, Karen. . . . Poor Emily. How awful to have ears full of fluid."

I left the room.

At dinner that night, Elizabeth said, "I wonder how Emily will feel when she's in hospital. I'm worried. She'll probably be scared to death."

"Maybe one of us can spend the night with her," suggested Nannie.

I hoped it would be Nannie or Elizabeth, not Daddy.

"I was scared when I had my tonsils out," said Charlie. "Remember?"

I stood up and announced, "We learned

26

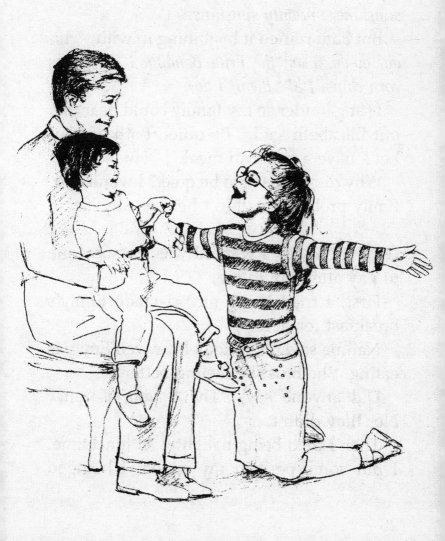

a new song in our music lesson this week. Do you want to hear it?" Before anyone could answer, I began singing, *"You are my sunshine, my only sunshine."*

But Sam ruined it by joining in with, *"Ay, ay, ay-ay. I am the Frito Bandito. I like Fritos corn chips. I like them, I do—"*

I sang louder so my family could hear me, but Elizabeth said, "Be quiet, both of you. Let's have a peaceful meal."

Why did we have to be quiet? I wondered. Emily probably couldn't hear us anyway.

On Sunday, all I wanted was for someone to pay attention to me.

First, I tried being nice. I made Emily's breakfast for her.

Nannie said, "Oh, look how well Emily is eating. She must be feeling better."

Did anyone say, "Thank you, Karen?" No, they didn't.

Then I tried being naughty. At lunchtime, I put some peas in my spoon. I boinged them across the table and they landed on the tray of Emily's high chair.

"Oh, what a mess," said Elizabeth. "Don't worry, Emily. I'll clean it up for you."

Later that afternoon, I waited until the food had settled in my stomach. Then I ran into the living room, where Daddy, Elizabeth, and Nannie were sitting. For once, Emily wasn't with them.

"Hey, everybody! Look at me!" I cried. I did a handstand, but I fell over.

"Karen," said Daddy, "is your bag packed? You and Andrew need to be ready to leave when Mummy comes."

I sat up slowly.

"It's packed," I said grumpily.

Then I stalked out of the living room.

I couldn't wait to go back to the little house.

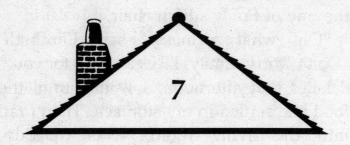

7

A Pet for Karen

When Andrew and I were back at the little house that night, I felt sad.

I sat on my bed for a while and just looked at Goosie. I didn't even talk to him.

Then I sat on a chair in our study. I swung my feet back and forth. I didn't turn on the TV.

Andrew came into the study and said, "Can I watch *Captain Tornado*?" He knows I hate *Captain Tornado*.

"I don't care," I answered.

I wished Midgie would push his wet nose into my hand, or that Rocky would curl up in my lap. But Rocky and Midgie were fast asleep on the rug in the utility room.

When Andrew turned on Captain Tornado I went back up to my bedroom. After a while, Mummy and Seth came in. They sat down next to me.

"Karen," said Mummy, "I don't think you had a very happy weekend at Daddy's, did you?"

I nodded.

"Do you want to tell us about it?" asked Seth.

"All anyone talks about over there is Emily. Emily this. Emily that. Emily, Emily, Emily. Sometimes I was lonely this weekend."

"You know Daddy still loves you, though, don't you?" asked Mummy. "And Elizabeth and Kristy and your brothers all love you, too."

"I suppose so," I replied. "But I didn't feel as if they loved me."

Seth put his arm around me and Mummy kissed my cheek.

"Do you know what I wish?" I said.

"What?" asked Mummy and Seth.

"I wish I had a pet of my own. I wish I had something that belonged to me, something I could take care of that would love me as much as I loved it. Hannie has Pat, and David Michael has Shannon."

Mummy and Seth looked at each other. They raised their eyebrows.

"Well," said Mummy after a moment, "I think you are probably old enough to have a pet."

"Really!" I cried.

"Really," Mummy answered. "If you promise to take care of your pet yourself — except for when you're at Daddy's. Then Seth and I will be happy to take care of it for you."

"Oh! Oh, goody, goody, goody! I can't believe it!" I exclaimed. Then I remembered to add, "Thank you. I promise to care for my pet. I'll never forget."

"There's just one thing though," said Seth. "You'll have to get a small pet. We don't want any more dogs or cats. We already have Rocky and Midgie. Another dog or cat would be too much trouble. But you can choose whatever kind of small pet you want."

"Can I have a pet, too?" asked a voice from the doorway. It was Andrew. He looked pleadingly at Mummy and Seth.

"When you're six," Mummy told him gently.

I was feeling so happy that I said to Andrew, "You can share my pet sometimes, okay?"

"Okay!"

Then Mummy and Seth and Andrew left me alone. I began to think. What kind of pet did I want? A hamster or a gerbil? No, they're too small. A rabbit? Maybe. A snake? No, they're horrid. Fish? No, they aren't any fun. A frog? Not very cuddly. It was too bad that I couldn't get a cat or dog. What I wanted was a cat of my own like Pat. But at least I was going to get a pet.

When I fell asleep that night I dreamed of animals.

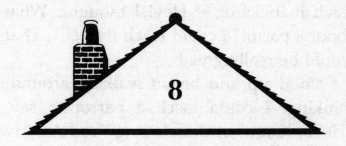

The Baby Bird

On Monday afternoon after school, I was still thinking about pets. I put my jacket on and wandered around the garden. I sat down on a rock.

What kind of pet? What kind of pet? I wondered. A mouse? No, *much* too small. A tortoise? No, even less cuddly than a frog, although it would be fun to watch a tortoise hide in its shell. A guinea pig? Maybe. But if I were going to get a guinea pig, I might as well get a rabbit. In playschool, our class pet was a rabbit called Nibbles, and I really liked him.

A clever animal would be fun. I could teach it tricks or — Hey! I thought. What about a parrot? I could teach it to *talk*. That would be really great!

I stood up and began walking around, thinking. I could teach a parrot to say, "Hello, Karen" or even to sing "You Are My Sunshine". We could sing together — Karen Brewer and her famous singing parrot.

I was thinking so hard about being famous that I wasn't watching where I was going. I nearly stepped on something in the grass. The something was alive.

"Yikes!" I cried.

I jumped back.

Then I bent down to see what it was.

It was a baby bird flopping around and looking scared. I didn't think it was hurt, but it seemed awfully small. Maybe it had fallen out of its nest. That happens sometimes.

Where was the bird's mother? I wondered. Then I remembered something that Miss Colman had told our class. Miss Colman is

our teacher, and she is very clever and nice. Miss Colman had said that if a mother or father animal smells the scent of·a human on its baby, it will abandon the baby. It will leave the baby for ever.

I didn't want that to happen to this baby, so I backed away. I sat down on the rock again and watched the bird. I waited for its mother or father to come swooping out of the sky and rescue it.

No big bird came.

But Rocky appeared. I saw him amble around the corner of the house. Uh—oh! I would have to rescue the bird myself. I ran into the kitchen to get a pair of oven gloves. I hoped I could get back to the bird before Rocky saw him.

Luckily I did. Rocky was sitting by the porch. I dashed past him and scooped the bird up in the gloves. The bird squawked wildly and flapped its tiny wings. But I managed to carry it inside.

"Mummy!" I cried. "Andrew! Come and see what I've found!"

Mummy and Andrew ran into the kitchen.

"What is it?" asked Mummy.

"A baby bird. I found it in the grass. I think it fell out of its nest. I was waiting for its mother to get it, but then Rocky came into the garden. I had to rescue it. What should we do with it?"

"Let's just make it comfortable for now," said Mummy. "We'll fix it up in a shoe box. Then we'll wait for Seth to come home from work. He'll know what to do. Seth is good with animals."

So Andrew and I put some soft rags and a cup of water in the shoe box. We put the bird on the rags. Then we waited for Seth.

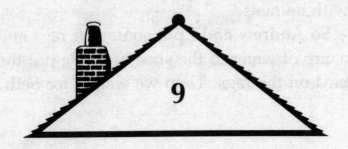

An Important Job

Seth didn't come home for two more hours. The bird squawked and flapped in the little box. It didn't look very happy.

Squawk, squawk, squawk.

Flap, flap, flap.

I felt sorry for the bird. It looked the way I felt when I didn't want to go to the dentist.

"Ssh, birdie," I said.

But the bird wouldn't be quiet.

I started to feel annoyed. I wanted to help the bird, but I didn't know how.

"Mummy?" I asked. "May I pat the bird?"

"I suppose so," Mummy answered. "Be very gentle."

I stroked the bird's feathers. "It's all right," I told the bird. "You'll feel better soon."

I was very happy when Seth finally came home.

"Seth! Seth! Look what I found in the garden!" I held the box out towards him. "What should we do? Mummy said you would know."

"Well," Seth replied slowly, "we can take care of the bird, but it will be an important job. Are you ready to help with an important job?"

"I'm ready," I said, feeling important.

"It's a good thing the bird is not hurt," said Seth. "It's just a little young. Still, it will need lots of care. All the care its mother would have given it."

Seth got busy collecting things — an eye syringe, some water, some grass and leaves and rags, and more.

"Do you think the bird is a boy or a girl?" I asked Seth.

Seth scratched his head. "I don't know," he replied.

"Well, I think it's a boy," I said, "so we can start calling the bird a 'him'."

Seth grinned, then he made a nest for the bird out of the grass and leaves and rags. Next he showed me the special food that he had made for the bird. He sucked it into the eye syringe.

"Now, Karen," he said, "baby birds eat very often. We will have to feed your bird every two hours or so. All day and all night for a while. Just like this."

Seth showed me how to feed the bird with the eye syringe. Straight away, the bird seemed happier. It settled down and stopped squawking so much. I thought of Emily. She had stopped crying after Dr Dellenkamp had given her the medicine for her ear. Emily and the bird were a bit alike. They needed big people to help them with some things.

I was glad my bird felt better.

"Karen?" said Mummy. "Do you think

you can remember to feed the bird every two hours after school? Seth and I will help you at night and while you're at school, but the rest of the time, he is your responsibility."

I nodded. "I can do it. I want to help the bird grow up. By the way, you don't have to get me a pet now. The bird will be my pet. You know why? I had just decided that the pet I would ask for was a parrot. And then I almost stepped on the bird. So the bird will be my pet instead. Okay?"

Mummy and Seth glanced at each other, but they didn't say anything.

"Squawk!" went the bird.

"Oh, you're so lovely, little birdie," I said, "I will have to name you. Then I can call you something besides 'him' and 'birdie'."

I looked happily into the bird's box. At last I had a pet of my own.

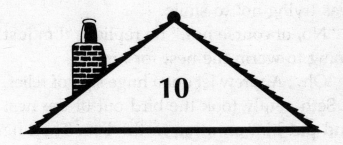

Magic Softee

Not long after the bird's first feed, Seth said, "Oh, I've just remembered! Baby birds are used to warm nests. Their mothers keep the nests warm and so do their brothers and sisters. This little chap must be getting chilly. We'll have to warm him up."

Seth turned on the oven and opened the door.

"You're going to cook the birdie?" shrieked Andrew.

"Oh, no, darling. Of course not," Mummy answered.

Seth looked around at us. I could tell he was trying not to smile.

"No, of course not," he replied. "I'm just going to warm the nest for him."

"Oh." Andrew let out a huge sigh of relief.

Seth gently took the bird out of the nest and put him on a rag in the box. Then he put the nest in the oven. He left it there for ten minutes. Then he put it back in the bird's box.

I touched it carefully. It wasn't too hot — just nice and warm.

Seth put the bird in the nest. The bird fell asleep straight away, I suppose he needed naps like Emily.

"Thank you, Seth," I said.

"That's all right," he replied. "But remember we still have a lot of work to do."

Why do grown-ups make everything seem like a chore? I wondered. I didn't mind feeding my bird and warming his nest.

A little while later, the bird woke up. He began to squawk again.

46

"Feeding time!" announced Seth, even though we were in the middle of our own dinner.

"Okay," I said. I stood up, found the eye syringe and filled it with food. Then I sat on the floor next to the bird's box and fed him the way Seth had shown me.

The bird grew quiet. I stroked his soft feathers. I felt just like his mother. I was feeding him and taking care of him and making him happy.

When the eye syringe was empty, the bird hopped into his nest and went to sleep again.

"Now I'll have to name the bird," I told Mummy, Seth and Andrew. We were clearing up the kitchen. "He needs a really good name. I'm going to go to my room to think, and I'll take the bird with me. That way, I can close my door and Rocky won't be able to get him."

So I carried the box and the syringe and the food upstairs. I put the box at the foot of my bed, closed the door and knelt by the box.

"What should I call you?" I asked the bird. (He was still asleep.) "I think I should call you after something I like."

I made a list of things I like:

Magic tricks
Roller- skating
Cats
Dogs
All animals
Mr Softee, the ice-cream man
Andrew and Kristy and
my families

I looked at the list. I couldn't call the bird Roller Skates and I couldn't call him Cat or Dog. Then I had a great idea. I could name him after two things I like. I would call him Magic Softee. That was a very, very special name. I hoped the bird would like it.

I wrote his name on his box and put the box on the radiator so Magic Softee could stay warm and comfy during the night.

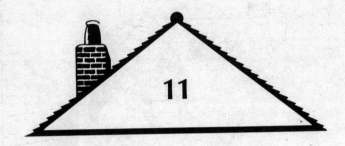

The Best Bird
in the Whole World

All that night, whenever Magic Softee squawked, Mummy or Seth or I would get up and feed him. He squawked six times, so each of us got up twice.

The next morning, I felt very sleepy. But I was glad to see that Magic Softee looked fine. He hopped around in his box and even chirped a couple of times.

"What kind of bird do you think Magic Softee is?" I asked Seth as he drove me to school.

"I think he's a sparrow," Seth replied. "He probably won't grow into a very big bird."

"That's all right," I said, "because he is the best bird in the whole world. . . Seth?"

"Yes?"

"Did you notice that I remembered to warm Magic Softee's nest before we left? And tonight I'll put it on the radiator again."

"I'm very proud of you," said Seth. He smiled at me.

"And Magic Softee seemed much happier today. He was hopping everywhere."

"You're doing a good job and being very responsible."

Seth dropped me off in front of my school and I ran straight to my classroom. A few other children were already there as well as Miss Colman, who was sitting at her desk.

"Guess what! Guess what!" I shouted.

"Karen," said Miss Colman gently. "Use your indoor voice."

51

"Sorry," I said. I put my things away in my locker. Then I joined Hannie and Nancy. They were talking to Natalie Springer and Ricky Torres in the back of the classroom.

"Guess what?" I said to them in a quieter voice. "I found a lost bird yesterday, so I put it in a box, and we've made a nest for it. We have to feed it about every two hours, and I've called it Magic Softee!"

"That's great!" said Natalie.

"What kind of name is Magic Softee?" asked Ricky.

I made a face at him. Ricky is a real pain.

A few more children came into the room. Nancy told them about Magic Softee. Everyone gathered around me and they all had lots of questions. I just love being in the middle of things and answering questions.

As soon as I got home that day, I ran to Magic Softee's box. He was fluttering around, chirping happily.

"Aah, you're so sweet, Magic Softee," I told him, stroking his feathers. "I love you. Do you know that?"

Mummy came into my room.

"How was he today?" I asked.

"Full of beans," said Mummy. "He seems to love his food."

"Well, I'll take over now," I said importantly. "Oh, Mummy, I'm so glad to have a pet at last."

Mummy looked thoughtful. "One day soon he will learn to fly, Karen," she said.

But I wasn't listening. I was gathering up Magic Softee's nest so I could warm it for him again.

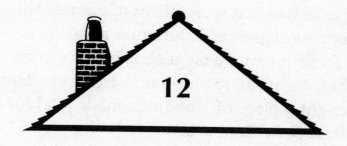

12

Show and Share

I found Magic Softee on Monday. All that week, he changed. He got a little bigger, he ate more, but not as often, and he hopped around more. He chirped more and squawked less. I thought I was being a very good mummy to Magic Softee.

On Thursday, Seth said to me, "It's time to move Magic Softee into a bigger box. And we'll have to cover it with a screen. Otherwise, he might escape and fly around the house. Have you noticed that he's trying to learn to fly?"

"Yes," I said, even though I hadn't noticed at all. I had just seen that Magic Softee was hopping higher and fluttering more.

So Seth found a bigger box in our garage. Then he went to the hardware shop. He bought a piece of wood and made a lid for Magic Softee's new box.

Every Monday, Wednesday, and Friday, we have Show and Share time in Miss Colman's class. You only have to tell something or bring something to show if you want to. I almost always have something for Show and Share.

Guess what I brought to school on Friday? Magic Softee! Actually, Mummy brought him. She brought him just for Show and Share, and she took him home straight afterwards. I didn't tell Hannie or Nancy or anyone except Miss Colman what I was going to do.

I was very excited about my surprise.

At Show and Share time on Friday, Miss Colman said, "Okay, boys and girls, who has something to show or share?"

Seven children raised their hands. I was one of them.

Then Miss Colman said, "I know what Karen has to show us, and it will be a surprise. It should be here any minute. While we wait, Ricky, why don't you share something with us?"

Ricky got up and stood in front of the class. All he had to show was a tooth he had lost. The stupid Tooth Fairy had given him a dollar for it.

Ricky was just sitting down when there was a knock on the door. Miss Colman opened it and there was Mummy carrying Magic Softee in his box! When she walked into the room, everyone said "Oooh!"

I stood proudly at the front of the class. Mummy put Magic Softee's box on a desk. Then she sat down in the visitor's chair.

"This," I said, "is Magic Softee. He's a baby sparrow. I found him on Monday, and I've been feeding him and warming his nest and —"

"I can't see!" cried Audrey. Audrey sits in the third row.

"Neither can I!" said Hannie and Nancy and lots of the other children.

"Then if you're very quiet," began Miss Colman, "you may all come to the front of the room. Remember to tiptoe and whisper."

"And I can take the lid off the box," I added.

My friends followed Miss Colman's directions. They crowded around Magic Softee, but they were very quiet.

"What do you feed him?" asked Ricky Torres.

"How much does he weigh?" asked Audrey.

"Do you ever let him outside?" asked Natalie Springer.

"What do Rocky and Midgie think of him?" asked Hannie.

"What will you do when Magic Softee learns to fly?" asked Miss Colman.

I answered everyone's questions — everyone's except Miss Colman's. Why did

adults keep talking to me about Magic Softee and flying?

I didn't want to think about that.

Instead I looked at all my friends. I pretended that they were a big audience and they had come to see Karen Brewer and her World-Famous Sparrow.

I just love being the centre of attention.

Someday I will be very famous.

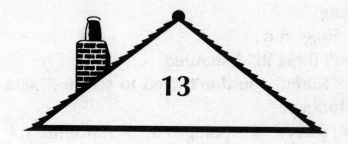

Kristy's Call

One thing I don't like about being Karen Two-Two is that I don't get to see my big-house family very often.

Kristy doesn't like this, either, so she said to me one day, "Let's talk on the phone sometimes when you're at your mum's house."

Now we usually talk once or twice a week.

One Wednesday — the Wednesday after Magic Softee had visited school, and two days before Andrew and I were supposed to go back to the big house — the phone rang.

Ring, ring.

"I'll get it!" I shouted.

"Karen, you don't need to scream," said Mummy.

"Sorry," I apologized. I ran into the kitchen.

I picked up the phone. "Hello, this is Karen Brewer," I said. I was going to say, "Hello, this is the *famous* Karen Brewer," but Mummy was in the kitchen, too. So I didn't.

"Hi, Karen. It's me, Kristy."

"Kristy!" I cried. Mummy and I looked at each other. I remembered to keep my voice down. "Hi!" I said. "Guess what. I took Magic Softee outside today. I mean, I took him outside in his box."

"Did he like going outside?" asked Kristy.

Kristy already knew about Magic Softee, since I had talked to her twice the week before. She knew how I had found him. She knew that he was growing, and that he had a new, bigger box.

"He liked it a lot, I think," I told Kristy. "Do you know what? I took the lid off so he could look around, and he flapped his wings and jumped right up onto the edge of the box. Then he just perched there."

"Weren't you afraid he would fly away?" asked Kristy.

"No," I replied. "'Course not. Why would he fly away? I'm his mother. Thanks to me, he feels a lot better. He chirps and eats and jumps around and he doesn't squawk any more."

"That's great" said Kristy. "Do you know who else feels better?"

"Who?"

"Emily. The medicine worked. Her ear infection is gone, and she isn't crying any more. Well, of course, sometimes she cries a little bit, but not the way she did when you were here the last time. That was really awful." (I was glad to hear Kristy say that.) "On Friday she goes into hospital. I'm sure she'll be scared, but once the tubes are in her ears, she'll *really* feel better."

64

"Who's going to stay at the hospital with Emily on Friday night?" I asked. I just had to know. *Please, please, please not Daddy.*

"My mum is," replied Kristy.

What a relief, I thought. But then I began imagining Emily staying in hospital. I thought of her lying in a strange bed. I thought of all the doctors and nurses coming into her room. They would probably give her injections and look in her ears and make her take medicine. Emily wouldn't understand what was going on. I began to feel a bit sorry for her, and I felt guilty for having been so cross with her before.

"Kristy," I said, "what will Emily think when she has to stay in hospital and have an operation?"

"I'm not sure," Kristy replied. "I'm a little worried. After all, she lived in an orphanage until she was two. Then she was taken away from the only place she'd known, and brought to a strange country and a strange family. Now we're going to take her to another strange place where some strange people are going to do things to her that will probably hurt."

"Yes," I said slowly.

Now I really felt terrible. I had yelled at Emily and called her a bad girl when she wasn't even feeling well.

I would have to do something to make up for it.

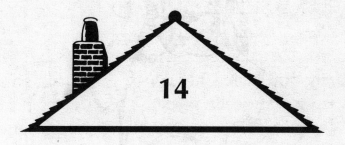

Get Well Soon, Emily

As soon as Kristy and I got off the phone, I went upstairs to my room. I felt like crying, but I wasn't sure why.

"Something's wrong," I said to Goosie. "I feel awful. Emily is a pain and she gets lots of attention, but she has to go to hospital, where she will be scared. She won't know what's happening to her. How could I have called her a pain when she is going to be so upset?"

Goosie wanted to say something to me, so I held him up to my ear and listened.

"What?" I said. "A card? A get-well card for Emily? Well, maybe I should make her one." I looked over at Magic Softee, who was hopping around in his box. "I could draw a picture of Magic Softee for Emily," I said, "couldn't I?"

I made Goosie nod his head.

"Okay, then. I'd better get to work."

I found some plain white paper in my desk. Then I found some crayons and felt-tips and glitter and glue. I put everything on the table in my room. I was ready to get to work.

First I folded a piece of paper in half. With the brown felt-tip, I drew the outline of a bird. I left plenty of space under him so I would have room to write. Then I spread glue all over the bird and sprinkled glitter on the glue. When I had finished, I had made a green bird with a red wing and a blue beak. I thought it was beautiful.

The bird didn't look anything like Magic Softee. Even so, at the bottom of the card I wrote:

THIS IS MY BIRD. HIS NAME IS MAGIC SOFTEE. MAGIC SOFTEE AND I HOPE THAT YOU WILL

I stopped writing there. I opened up the card. Inside I wrote:

GET WELL SOON!

I made each letter a different colour. Then I signed my name in joined-up writing!

Love, Karen

"Here, Goosie," I said. "Look at this."

I showed Goosie the card and made him nod his head again and say in a little cat voice, "Very pretty, Karen."

Then I remembered something. I remembered how I had felt when I came home from hospital with my broken wrist. I had been bored. Emily would probably be bored, too. So I found a colouring book that I had only coloured one page in. I would give Emily the card and the book on Saturday.

I felt a little bit better about having been so mean to Emily.

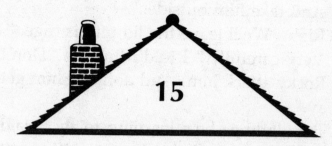

15

Big Sisters, Little Sisters, Middle Sisters

Two days later it was another going-to-Daddy's Friday. As Andrew and I were packing our bags, I said to Mummy, "What will happen to Magic Softee while I'm gone?"

"Seth and I will take care of him," Mummy replied. "We told you we would care for any pet you got whenever you're at Daddy's. Remember?"

I nodded. "Don't forget to change his water."

"We won't."

"Or to feed him."

"Of course not."

"And take him outside."

"Right. We'll leave the lid off his cage."

"Very carefully," I told Mummy. "Don't let Rocky attack him. And don't let him get away."

"But darling, he's learning to fly," said Mummy. "He needs his freedom. We can't keep him cooped up in a box all his life — he's a wild bird."

I thought for a long time. Finally I said, "Well, Magic Softee won't fly away and leave me because I'm his mother."

When Andrew and I got to the big house, Daddy and Elizabeth and Emily had already left. They were at the hospital. Nannie was in charge, and Kristy and all my brothers were at home.

"This isn't too bad," I said to Andrew. We were going upstairs to unpack our bags. "It's just like any night when Daddy and Elizabeth go out and Nannie or Kristy babysits for us."

"Yes," replied Andrew. "Except that Emily isn't here."

"I know," I said. I couldn't work out why I felt disappointed.

After I had unpacked, I put Emily's card and colouring book on my desk so that I would remember to give them to her the next day.

At supper that night I said to Nannie, "When will Emily have her operation?"

"First thing tomorrow morning," Nannie

answered. "It won't take very long. Emily will be ready to come home after lunch. In fact, anyone who wants to can go to the hospital to pick her up. You can even go to her ward."

"Right up to her *ward*?" said Andrew.

"That's great!" said David Michael.

"Yes," said Kristy, Sam and Charlie.

I had a feeling we would all be going to the hospital the next day.

When bedtime came that night, Andrew and David Michael and I brushed our teeth together. We foamed up the toothpaste in our mouths. Then, "Unh, two, fee, pit!" I said with my full mouth.

We spat into the sink and looked at all the foam. There was quite a lot of it.

Afterwards, Kristy read me a bedtime story. It was called *A Baby Sister for Frances*. "You know," said Kristy, when the story was over, "now that Emily is here, my brothers and I have two little sisters — you and Emily."

"But I'm not the littlest little sister any more," I said.

"No," Kristy replied, "but you're still my first little sister. Also, you're something else that is very special. You're a middle sister, which means you're an older sister and a younger sister. Emily will probably never get to be a middle sister."

I thought about that. Then I said, "You know what, Kristy?"

"What?"

"I love you."

"I love you, too."

"Goodnight, big sister."

"Goodnight, middle sister."

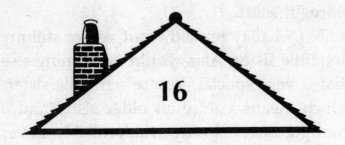

In the Hospital

The next day was Emily Day. In the morning, Daddy drove to the hospital to stay with Emily and Elizabeth.

Before he left, Nannie said to him, "The rest of us will come at two-thirty so we can all be there when the doctor says Emily can come home."

I didn't like to admit it, but I was excited about going to the hospital. I had never been in a hospital ward — not the kind where you spend the night. I wanted to see what one looked like. And I wanted to see

Emily and Elizabeth — especially Emily. I wanted to make sure she wasn't too scared, and I wanted to show her that I was sorry I had called her a bad girl and been cross with her.

At two-fifteen, Nannie called, "Everybody into the Pink Clinker! I'm driving!"

Sam and Charlie groaned. They're embarrassed to be seen in Nannie's rattly old pink car, but I like the Pink Clinker.

I grabbed the get-well card I had made for Emily and raced outside to the car. I scrambled into the back seat. Kristy, Sam, Andrew and David Michael crawled in after me and Charlie climbed into the front seat.

We all put on our seat belts.

"Off we go!" said Nannie.

Sam and Charlie ducked down and wouldn't sit up straight until we reached the hospital.

As we were getting out of the car I said, "The last time I was here was when I had my plastercast off."

"Really?" said Sam. "I thought the last

time you were here was when you had that brain operation. The one that made you so weird."

"Oh, *Sam*," I said.

Nannie led us into the hospital, and in no time at all we were walking through the doorway to Emily's ward. I was surprised to see Emily standing up in her cot.

"Hi, Emily!" we said.

Emily just looked at us for a few moments. Then she gave us a huge smile.

She knows us! I thought. She knows *me*. She remembers me and likes me. I felt the way I felt when I would kneel by Magic Softee's box and he would hop over to me.

Andrew and David Michael began exploring Emily's ward. It was pretty ugly and boring except for a TV set mounted way up high in a corner. That was quite interesting. Sam, Charlie and Kristy talked to each other, and Daddy and Elizabeth and Nannie talked to a doctor who had come into the ward.

So I talked to Emily. I stood by her bed

and read the get-well card to her.

"Look," I said. "This is Magic Softee. He's my bird. He's a sparrow. Maybe you can see him sometime. Okay?"

"Da," said Emily. (We're not sure what "da" means.)

I tickled Emily's toes. She giggled.

Then Elizabeth said, "Okay, everybody. We can go home now. Let's get the show on the road."

Nannie and Elizabeth put Emily's things in a little bag. Kristy lifted Emily out of her cot. And Daddy picked *me* up and said, "Thank you for making Emily the card. That was nice of you. I'm very proud of you."

I kissed Daddy on his head, right on the place where he's going bald.

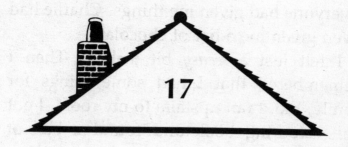

Karen's Little Sister

As soon as we got home, Elizabeth settled Emily on the couch in the study. She put her pillow there and covered her with a blanket. David Michael turned on the TV and found a cartoon show that Emily likes. Kristy gave Emily her favourite stuffed animal, a poodle called Pooh, Elizabeth gave Emily her favourite book, *Caps for Sale* and Charlie gave her a piece of chocolate.

This was just like when I had come home from casualty with the plastercast on my arm. I had stretched out on the couch and

David Michael had turned on the TV. Everyone had given me things. Charlie had even given me a bar of chocolate.

I felt just a *teensy* bit jealous. Then I remembered that I had some things for Emily, too. I ran upstairs to my room. I got the colouring book and found a box of crayons. I took a secret surprise out of my bag. Then I ran back to the study.

"Here, Emily," I said. "These are for you."

Emily was rubbing her ears again. She looked as if she might cry. But when I sat down next to her, she stopped rubbing her ears and she even smiled.

"Da?" she said.

"Crayon," I told her, taking a red one out of the box. "Crayon."

"Cray," Emily said.

Then I opened the colouring book. "See?" I said. "You can colour all these pictures."

Emily knows what crayons are for, but she's not a very good colourer yet. She scribbled all over a picture of a kitten. Then she handed the book back to me. "Kitty," she said.

"That's right!" I exclaimed. "That is a kitty. Good girl, Emily! Hey, Emily, I have something else for you," I said. I took the secret something from where I'd hidden it behind a cushion. I opened up an envelope.

"These," I said, "are *real* pictures of Magic Softee. See him, Emily? That's my bird."

"Bird," repeated Emily.

"Yes. Good girl!"

After I had shown Emily the photos, she began to look tired. "Everybody leave the study!" I announced. "Emily needs a nap."

I tucked the blanket around my little sister. Kristy and my brothers tiptoed out of the study. Emily was already falling asleep.

I felt grown up. I liked taking care of Emily the way I took care of Magic Softee. But I didn't like watching Daddy and Elizabeth and Kristy and everyone spend so much time with her. Daddy bought her a pink pig, which Emily named Piggy. Kristy spent

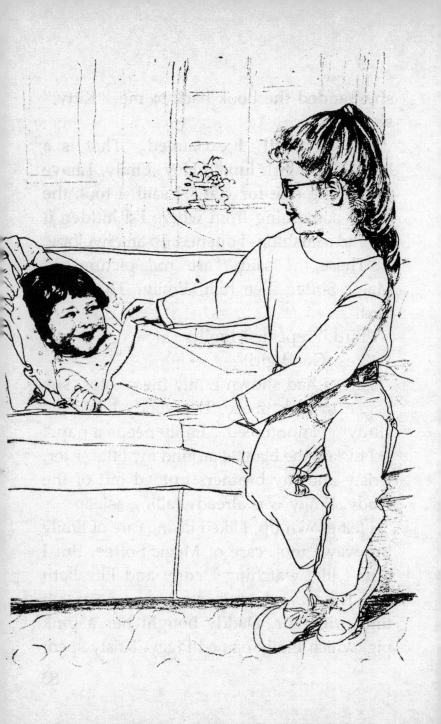

lots of time reading books to Emily that afternoon, and Charlie gave her another piece of chocolate.

Still, I knew how they felt. I had given her the colouring book and crayons and card, and shown her the pictures of Magic Softee. Also, I was glad Emily didn't seem too frightened after being in the hospital. She just seemed happy to be home with us again.

And at bedtime that night, Kristy and I read together for half an hour.

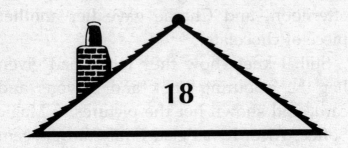

Where Is Magic Softee?

On Sunday morning, Emily was much better. She woke up early and Elizabeth dressed her and took her downstairs for breakfast in her high chair.

I could tell it was going to be a normal day.

Except for one thing. I was beginning to worry about Magic Softee.

It started when we were finishing breakfast and Emily suddenly called out, "Bird?"

Daddy, Elizabeth, Nannie, Sam and I were still sitting at the table in the kitchen.

We turned and looked out of the window. Sure enough, a bird was sitting on the bird table. It was a sparrow, like Magic Softee.

In fact, for just a moment, I thought it *was* Magic Softee. Then I saw that the bird was bigger than my pet. But that was when the worrying started. I wondered if Mummy and Seth were being careful when they took Magic Softee outside. Were they keeping Rocky indoors? What if they let Magic Softee hop out of his box? Would he start to fly?

I worried so much that I wanted to phone Mummy. But I didn't. I didn't want Mummy to think I didn't trust her.

Instead, I just kept worrying.

Magic Softee wouldn't leave me. . . would he? He was my special pet. I had saved his life – he must know that. But what if he was gone when I returned to the little house?

All day I was nice to Emily, and all day I worried.

When Mummy and Seth finally pulled up in front of Daddy's house, I ran out to their car.

"Goodbye!" I called to my big-house family.

I didn't even stop to kiss or hug anyone. I just slid into the car. "Is Magic Softee okay?" I asked.

Andrew climbed in next to me.

"He's fine, honey," said Mummy.

"Where is he?"

"Around somewhere," said Seth. "Don't worry."

"What do you mean 'around somewhere'?"

"You'll see when we get home," Mummy answered.

As soon as our car was parked by the little house, I scrambled out, dropped my bag, and ran to the back garden.

There was Magic Softee's box. I looked inside. It was empty.

"Mummy! Seth!" I called. "Magic Softee is gone! You let him escape!"

I was about to start crying when I heard a chirp. I looked up. Magic Softee was perched on the edge of the porch roof.

"How did he get up there?" I asked Seth.

He had come running into the garden.

"He flew. He's been flying a lot this weekend. To the bird table, even to the branch of a tree. He hardly uses his box any more."

Suddenly I knew the truth. It was awful. "Magic Softee isn't going to be my pet any more, is he?" I said.

Mummy had joined us in the garden. "I think he's going to stick around," she said.

"He just won't need his box. He's going to be on his own. He is wild, you know."

I nodded. I understood. Magic Softee wouldn't leave — but he wasn't going to be my special pet, either.

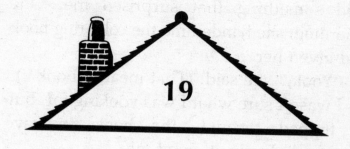

19

Softee Bird

Two weeks went by, and guess what? Magic Softee didn't leave. He really didn't. He never used his box again, but he was always in our garden.

He perched in the branches of our trees. He ate from the bird-table. He splashed in the bird-bath. He learned how to stay away from Rocky.

I could tell him from all the other birds in the garden.

He was my bird, but he wasn't my pet.

The next time I was at Daddy's house, Emily did something that surprised me. One morning, she handed me the colouring book I'd given her.

"Yook," she said. (That means "Look".)

I wasn't sure what I was yooking for, but I flipped through the book anyway. Suddenly Emily stopped me.

"Bird!" she announced triumphantly.

Sure enough, she had scribbled over a picture of a bird that looked like Magic Softee.

"You bird," she said.

"My bird?" Did Emily really remember Magic Softee? I was surprised.

And then I had a good idea. I talked to Daddy about it and he thought my good idea was a great idea.

So Daddy and Kristy and Charlie and I arranged a special surprise for Emily. The surprise would take place on Monday, the day after Andrew and I went back to the little house.

In school on Monday I was very excited.

I couldn't wait for the afternoon. Miss Colman had to keep saying, "Karen, pay attention."

I tried to, but it wasn't easy.

At last, school was over and I was at home again. I looked at my watch three million times. (Not really.) I was waiting for four-thirty.

At four-thirty on the dot, Elizabeth's car stopped in front of our house. Charlie was driving it and Kristy was sitting next to him. Emily was in her car seat behind them.

When they got out of the car, I began to laugh. Emily was wearing a shirt that said, "I'm the little sister". Kristy was wearing a shirt that said, "I'm the big sister".

"There's one for you, too," she said. She handed me a shirt of my own. It read, "I'm the middle sister. . . and proud of it!"

I laughed. Then I said, "Come on, all of you. I'll show you Magic Softee." I took Emily by the hand. Kristy and Charlie and Emily and I walked to the back of the house.

I whistled my special whistle for Magic Softee.

A few moments later he swooped down from somewhere. He landed on a low tree branch.

I lifted Emily up to see him.

"There he is, Emily," I said. "There's Magic Softee. Can you say 'Magic Softee'? Can you say 'bird'?"

Emily paused. Finally she said, "Softee bird," and smiled.

I giggled. Little sisters can be fun. . . sometimes.

When Magic Softee flew away, I put Emily on the ground. "Okay, put on your new shirt," said Charlie.

"Why?" I asked.

"You'll see."

I ran inside and changed into the shirt.

When I went back outdoors, Charlie was holding a camera.

"Line up, you three," he said.

Kristy and Emily and I stood in a line.

Click! went the camera.

Now I keep a copy of the three-sisters picture on my mirror at the little house.

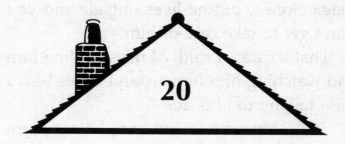

20

Emily Junior

Magic Softee had been a wild bird for more than a month when Mummy and Seth came into my room one night. I was sitting at my desk, wearing my blue glasses and doing my homework.

"Karen," said Mummy, "Seth and I have been thinking."

"We've been thinking hard," said Seth. "Our brains are aching."

I laughed. "Oh, Seth!"

"We were thinking," said Mummy, "that we promised you a pet of your own, but in the end, you didn't really get one. You have Magic Softee, but he lives outside and you don't get to take care of him."

"That's true," I said. "I miss feeding him and watching him hop around in his box. I miss talking to him, too."

"So," Mummy went on, "we were wondering if you would like to get another pet — a real pet — since Magic Softee isn't what you had in mind."

"Really?" I cried. I jumped up from my desk. "I can really get another pet? Oh, thank you, thank you, thank you!"

I threw my arms around Mummy. Then I gave Seth a big hug, too.

That night, when I'd finished my homework, I sat on my bed. I held Goosie in my lap.

"What kind of pet should I get?" I asked Goosie. "I don't think I want another bird. Or hamsters or mice or gerbils or fish. And Seth said no more cats or dogs."

Goosie looked like he had an idea. I held him up to my ear so he could whisper it to me.

"An animal from a book that I like?" I repeated. "That's a great idea! Let me see. There's Paddington, but I can't get a bear. And there's Ferdinand, but I can't get a bull. . . . Wait a minute! I loved Nicodemus in *Mrs Frisby and the Rats of NIMH*. He was a wonderful, kind, clever rat. That's it! I'll get a nice rat like Nicodemus. A rat will be small, but not too small."

I ran downstairs. "Mummy? Seth?" I said.

They were sitting in the living room. "Yes, darling?" said Mummy.

"I know what kind of pet I want. I want a rat like Nicodemus."

Mummy and Seth looked at each other. For just a second, I thought they were going to say, "No. No rats."

Instead, Mummy said, "We'll go to the pet shop tomorrow."

The man at the shop was very nice. He said, "We don't have any rats at the moment, but we can order one. It will take a week. Will that be all right?"

"Yes," I said. "That will be fine."

I didn't like waiting for a whole week. The week dragged by, but I knew that when it was over I would have a pet of my own at last.

The next Tuesday, Mummy drove Andrew and me to the pet shop. There was my rat. He was waiting in a cage. We bought him an aquarium as well as some cedar shavings, a water bottle and some special rat food.

As soon as we were home again, I got my rat's cage ready.

"This is your house," I told him. "You have everything you need. . . everything except a name," I added.

I thought and thought.

At last I said, "I'm going to call you Emily Junior, after my little sister."

And so I did.